RELAY
SHORT FICTIONS

Relay
Short Fictions

Betsy Struthers

for Terry Ann
with admiration
for the sharing of story

Betsy Struthers

Black Moss
2010 Press

Library and Archives Canada Cataloguing in Publication

Struthers, Betsy, 1951-
    Relay : short fictions / Betsy Struthers.

ISBN 978-0-88753-472-0

    I. Title.

PS8587.T7298R45 2010   C813'.54   C2010-902230-0

Cover photo: Marty Gervais
Design: Karen Veryle Monck

Published by Black Moss Press at 2450 Byng Road, Windsor, Ontario, N8W 3E8. Canada. Black Moss books are distributed in Canada and the U.S. by LitDistCo. All orders should be directed there.

Black Moss would like to acknowledge the generous financial support from both the Canada Council for the Arts and the Ontario Arts Council.

ONTARIO ARTS COUNCIL
CONSEIL DES ARTS DE L'ONTARIO

Le Conseil des Arts | The Canada Council
du Canada | for the Arts

PRINTED IN CANADA

for Bob and Wendy Struthers,
forty years

... but time and chance happen to them all

Ecclesiastes 9, 11

Contents

THE ROMANTIC

Arrives ten minutes late but the woman—girl, really—isn't here, first time she's kept him waiting.

Bartender—red hair buzz cut on top, long over the nape of her neck, white tee hiding nothing, nothing much to hide; wannabe boy in jeans and green apron—leans on his table, hip not quite touching his hand, so thin you'd miss her altogether if she stood sideways. Clicks a silver pen against her yellow teeth. Can smell the smoke on her.

Orders lager. Should have ordered wine, white wine, girls like to drink white wine. But a man deserves a beer though his job is in an office, not construction. Works as hard as father ever did. Tools a telephone, computer; last year top sales, fourth year running.

Lives the good life: condo on the lake, cottage in Muskoka where they're headed for the weekend. Looks at his watch—thin, gold, complicated dial—pours another glass. Not wrong to want a cold drink on a scorching day, expect your girl to share one with you. Expect your girl to be waiting.

Strokes his own bare skull, a nervous tic. Better to shave than comb-over. The skinhead desperado look. Black silk shirt, black jeans, three-day scruff of beard. Like an artist. Man living an artist's life.

At last. The girl—a woman, really—glasses sliding down her freckled nose; bangs pushed back, roots showing— pushes through the door, hesitates, haloed in light and traf- fic noise. Dress plastered to her body by the breeze, sandal straps that wrap around her calves, Roman slave-girl style.

Some other guy—at a table with three men who argue over papers while he sips the wine they're sharing—looks her up and down. Nods at him. He grins. After all, she's coming here for him. She's his.

She drops her purse on the banquette before sliding in, not close enough to touch, cradles the glass he hands her in both hands. Ring on her wedding finger. Thought she'd take that off. Bitten nails, raw cuticles.

Picture a pendant nestled in the hollow of that throat. Between the swell of breasts. Has bought a necklace for her, to give her in the morning. Picture her naked except for that gold strand, the heavy pearl. It's in his bag in the trunk of his Corvette. Receipt in his wallet. Reaches for her hand.

They once went out for drinks, husband out of town, musician, always on the road, she's supporting him until he makes it big. As if that's going to happen since it hasn't happened yet. So they had one or two too many. Drove her home, her head heavy on his shoulder. She didn't ask him in. Hugged in the shadow under a maple, its rusting leaves applauding. Had kissed her, long and hard. She kissed back. She had.

Grabs her hand but her fist is limp in his. Silly to hold on to her like this. He shouldn't have to beg. She didn't stop him when he put his arms around her then. She didn't say no a week ago beneath the whispering tree.

People from his office swagger in, two men and a woman—red jacket, short black skirt, stiletto heels. From here he sees black lace beneath the sheer cream of her blouse. She pouts her lips at him. Inviting.

The girl stands up and turns away. Foot hooks a chair

leg, sends it crashing. From the back, she's all sharp points, hunched shoulder blades, bony elbows crooked. One sandal strap comes loose, slaps the floor behind her. As if it waved goodbye. As if he were looking.

The Escape Artist

Hard to make a dignified exit when your shoe lace is un-done, flaps on the ground, ridiculous sandals, straps always slipping, tripping, like hobbles, like shackles.

Walk at least a block before stopping to bend down to tie the errant lace and DON'T LOOK BACK, see if he's following or not, saw the look he gave that woman wearing red.

Never *said* you'd go with him. And what about your husband? So what if he's too often on the road, he calls when he's away, he always comes back home. Lie in the bed you've made and like it.

And okay, yes, you kissed him back, you've been left too often to do for yourself what you can. If you could have stood there hugging, holding on. But he meant more than that of course and you ... don't know.

Go home, take a taxi, damn the cost. Go home, throw out these stupid shoes and have a drink. Have a drink or three. What it takes to get you through the night.

HER HUSBAND

If she could be here, could see. Times like this when the music's working, crowd close to the stage, fists pumping, the force of it, the energy, *okay*.

If she could see, she'd understand he has to have more time. She's got a job, she can make the rent. When he makes it big, he'll pay her back. With interest. And then see where he'll move them.

Bitch on bass stomps over, that glare, *get back in the chorus*. With the rest of them. Put in place.

Always wanted to be a known name. Needed. Not working for the man but for himself. Making music. Carried away. There's groceries and there's passion and there's hard work to get here in the spotlight. Won't have it taken off him, not just yet.

One more chance. He told his wife. He told the other members of the band. If he could channel what the music makes him feel, they'd call out for more. He *knows* this. Sure as the sun shines and the bear in the woods. He might not have all his shit together yet but what he's got is gold.

The Bass Player

Who does he think he is, God's gift? A star in his own eyes.

Whose songs pull them to their feet, get the encores, even in a bar like this? Not his. His the sloppy solos she has to cover up for and she does.

Making money—finally—gigs piling up, full calendar for the next six months at least. Tonight a guy from *Eye* is coming to review the band, that means national attention. And he, *God's gift*, struts around the stage as if he owns it.

She's had enough of men, not only him, her father phoning every day to talk about her sister—her perfect single life, perfect 9-to-5, perfect pension plan. She's never wanted anything but this. She won't be like her mother or his wife, taking what they give her.

There's the cue, their turn on stage. He's grabbed the mic already. Well. This will be his last time. It's her turn, she's on her way, she's coming out.

Her Sister

If she doesn't at least get the laundry done, then the day is worse than wasted. If she doesn't get the laundry done, she might as well call it quits.

Easy to get the laundry sorted and into the bundle buggy. Can't go to the machines in the basement, might meet a neighbour who will want to talk. Bad enough that her father keeps phoning. And sometimes her sister. She lets the machine answer, lets them think she's gone out. She's busy.

Hasn't been to the office in over a week. Over two weeks. They're asking for a doctor's note to say what she's sick with. She says one thing or another. She says anything to get them off the line. So she can lie back down. Even though she keeps the blinds down in the bedroom, in every room of the condo, light pours in. *Look at that light*, her sister said the only time she visited, but she's found out: light means shadows.

First she can't get on the bus any more, all those strangers' eyes. And in the office people stop talking when she goes by. Look away too quickly, won't send her replies. Her computer for no reason keeps crashing.

Okay.

Go down the hall, down the elevator, three floors, out the door, down the front steps. Turn left, two blocks to Sherbrooke, turn right, cross the road at the lights, laundromat between tourist agency—poster of white sand, blue sky, thatched cabins—and wine bar—*ladies' night Thursdays.*

She's opened her front door a million times. She can do this. Turn the knob. Pull. Go through. Close it behind her. Lock it.

She's got the IPod on shuffle: Amy Winehouse, Broken Social Scene, Modest Mouse. Her own music, not her sister's, not her sister's band. She could walk like this for hours watching feet propel her forward over cracks and curbs, drum beats shutting out the street. Shutting out the cars. The people.

Someone grabs her. Throws her down on concrete. Buggy spills over. Bladder spills over. Ear buds fall out, music ripped away. Something makes sounds like banging on pots.

Someone yells. Someone points at the window in the room above the laundry, says something about a man with a gun, police cars blocking the street. Somewhere sirens squawl.

What she's always known: someone is out to get her.

From high overhead, as if in an airplane, she looks down at the pile of clothes on the pavement. A woman who can't keep her dirty laundry to herself. A woman screaming at the cop who saves her. Scream and not stop screaming. No wonder people laugh.

She is not that person. She is on her way to the beach, to the sunshine, the crisp hotel sheets and warm salt water. They can do what they want with that thing. She's not here any more. She's left the building.

THE OFFICER

Omigod, citizen down, shot, somebody, help.

Call comes in, domestic gone haywire, everybody out, SWAT team, helicopter, damn newsies parking where they're in the way.

Back here controlling traffic, traffic for christ's sake, when all hell is breaking loose across the street and no one knows if the guy has shot his wife or if the kids are there, if there are kids, if she is his wife. In the window aiming at anything that moves. Not like it sounds on TV. More like his nephew on the floor in the kitchen with a wooden ladle and the soup pot upside down. Sister saying, *isn't it about time you had one of these?*

Where are the goddamn paramedics? Can't see any blood, but she's wet herself, she won't stop screaming. Nicely dressed, clean, cart full of laundry, towels and panties all over the sidewalk, should he pick them up? Laundromat across the street. What a thing for her to walk into.

All these gawkers. Old lady and her dog. Rat dog, white

with one black ear, black stump of tail. The teeth on it. Saw one rip the jaw of a boxer once, may be small but nasty.

Victim won't stop screaming. Curled like a baby, stain spreading on her jeans, fists clenched over open mouth. She could be dying, paramedics still not here.

To be in uniform and helpless.

Rifle arcs from the upstairs window, shatters on the street, cops in body armour swarm the building. It's all over. And hasn't had a chance to draw his gun.

THE HOSTAGE

Why did she open the door? Why did she let him in? At least he didn't arrive until the kids were off to school. They don't have to see him like this, don't have to listen to his bluster. But she won't let him take them, not even for a weekend, she knows it's likely he won't bring them back. Either run away with them or kill them all, he's threatened that so often. And the baby just turned six.

When his face went stiff, twitch at the corner of his eye, at least she knew enough to run into the bathroom, only room in the place she can lock. And push the hamper in front of it. And lie down in the empty tub, pull all the laundry over her. The shot came through the door at her heart's height.

Phone rings, he answers, shouts and swears. Sirens in the street. *Pop pop* of his gun. Where did he get a gun? When did he learn to shoot? *Pop pop*. There's screaming in the street and he's screaming and then the shooting stops. Five bullets. One for each of them. At least the kids are in school. At least the porcelain is cool on her cheek. She nestles deeper. It's over. They'll take him away for good this time. She'll be able to sleep without fearing he'll call, that he'll come back in the night. The kids in school. She could sleep now for a week.

The Dog-Walker

Come *on*, Jackie, walk *along*, Jackie, there's nothing for us *here*, Jackie.

What the world is coming to. *The world is too much with us*—who wrote that? Bible? Book of Common Prayer? Shakespeare? Wordsworth: *For this, for everything, we are out of tune.*

How rude that young man was, an officer of the law, making us move on. We only want to help, eh Jack? Poor woman. Shame to make a mess like that in public. I could give her, what? This sweater, cover up. Oh well.

Was a good place to live before all these apartments. Where real homes used to be. If only they had left it all alone. There I go. Woulda, coulda, shoulda. The past. Pluperfect.

What's past is so much clearer than the present. Let's not talk about the future. The past—it's got its beginning, middle, and its end, true narrative, all we want, a good story. Happily ever after.

What time is it? What time? *There will be time, there will be time.* Oh Eliot, oh Prufrock. Oh for the time before this time when he was here with me, held your leash in one hand, my hand in his other. First the children go, then him, then I will have to go, my daughter says, leave our house of many rooms to live in one.

How I will miss the light in the bedroom in the early morning before the kids wake up. Miss the creaking of our double bed.

The Witness

So you see that dog there? My uncle had a dog like that, only with a bit more brown in it. Same way it strains at the collar, almost strangles itself, wish it would, hate the things, I do. That dog bit everyone, some more than once. Good thing to visit in winter, thick coat, feel weight but no teeth, could knock you sideways off the porch, got the scar to prove it. See? Here? Felt those teeth in summer though. Yeah. My uncle and his dogs.

So, one time my cousin brings his girlfriend home. She brings her parrot with her, scrawny thing, but loud. Whistles up a storm. Drives the dog plum crazy. Cage on top of the buffet, dog springing like a jack on its hind legs. Oh, the barks and squawks.

So she lets the bird fly free when the dog's out in the yard. And of course the dog gets in, takes the parrot in mid-air, head first, and in the hall before she has a chance to scream.

Uncle, cousin, girlfriend, all us kids chase the dog around the house from kitchen to living room, back again, us laughing fit to burst. *It's not funny*, she yells at us, but all you can see of the bird is feet, dog gulping as it runs. Uncle swearing, *it's not dead, it's faking*.

So my aunt offers a chicken wing and that's enough to make the dog spit out what's left: not much but claws and feathers. Buried them at the foot of the garden. Dog digs them up three times before my uncle does the job proper. Their john won't flush right for a week. So a dog like that. Yeah. Let me tell you. I got a hundred stories.

The Uncle

Where is the goddamn jeezly car key?

Slams open, slams shut the top drawer of his desk, each of the kitchen drawers, the drawer in the telephone table in the hall. Sweeps his forearm over the table, knocks letters and a vase to the floor. Crystal hits the padded carpet and does not break, flowers silk, so nothing spills. Wants shards of glass and a dirty puddle. Wants her to step in it.

Pockets. Used to the weight of keys in his pants pocket, soft thud against his thigh each time he moves. Goes through the coat cupboard, the clothes cupboards, his and hers, checks every pocket, comes up empty. Not on any window sill, on top of the piano, on back of the commode.

She won't let him call her at work, can't take personal calls in the library. He knows why, he's seen her at the front desk smiling at the men and boys with their furtive books and rolled up magazines. Why she needs a job. At her age. His.

Where did you last put it? his mother would say about anything lost, baseball glove, schoolbag, Sunday school pin. A saint she was, may she rest in peace. *Close your eyes and picture where you were when you last saw it.* Good idea. Sit on the edge of the bed for a minute. Take a load off these weary feet. Take a breather.

Tugs the cord of the oxygen tank that follows him everywhere like a cur with its tail between its legs, a dog that doesn't know enough to run away from a beating. Hangdog. Tubes in his nose, hanging round his neck. Lies down, times his breathing to the pant of the machine.

Where was he when he last had the key? Weight settles on his chest, dog up on the bed resting her head there, eyes on his. Dogs, always underfoot, always begging for attention. This one, though. Would pat her silky fur.

Dog pants heavily, licks his face. Reaches up to brush her tongue away, cheeks wet and the tears keep leaking. In a minute, he'll get up. He'll get up and take the damn dog for a walk, drive to the park and let her run, chase sticks. Always had a good arm, good pitch. Time to go. In a minute, when he's caught his breath. When he can find the key.

THE GRASS WIDOW

When co-workers talk husband-and-wife, she says nothing. When one complains about her aging spouse, how she's had to take away his keys, how she's working only to get some time away from him and his demands, she can't admit that in fifteen years she's had only forty-six whole nights with her lover, mostly when his wife took the children to visit family in Vancouver. She could hardly sleep those hours he was in her bed.

When she treasures that one weekend in Niagara. The only photo he let her take was of the waters roiling in the gorge. Her desktop theme. When they have their Wednesday afternoons and Sunday mornings. When he's supposed to be *out with the boys* curling or playing golf. Some Wednesday mornings she's so giddy the Head Librarian says her head is in the clouds. She says *Sorry*. Though she never is. Even a text message from him makes her stutter.

When he doesn't come to the café at the hour appointed. His office says he's unavailable; he answers neither email nor cell phone. His married daughter picks up his home phone. *My mother*, she cries, *oh my father*.

When she drives by his house in the evening, sees the cars, the crowd at the door, women clutching kleenex and casseroles, men with their fists in their pockets. She has to wait for the morning obits, she has to read *suddenly* and *in the arms of his family*. She parks up the block from the funeral home, tails the hearse to the cemetery. When the sheets of her bed still smell of him. When he is the last to put gas in her car. When she sells the car, not wanting to go anywhere. Nowhere to go without him.

THE SYBIL

Call it superstition if you like: bird in the hand. Bird in the house. Birds of a feather. Bird brain to be upset when she finds a ball of feathers, hollow bones, among ashes in the chimney. Twice she has seen owls in daylight, the first time the day her father died, though she didn't know that then. She was driving down a county road lined by cedars and corn fields, snow falling gently. Out of nowhere it swooped across the hood, white wingspan masked her view. Car could have hit the ditch, rolled, smashed, she the broken yolk. She stopped dead, headlights picking out plow tracks. Silence. Empty woods. All she can do afterwards, to strangers calling on the phone and at the wake, is talk about the owl, the size of it, its grace. Like an angel or a ghost. And two hours later the phone call, so unexpected. The shock is with her still.

Second time, one of those ice-blue February mornings, the kind of morning she thinks about snow-shoeing with the dog, shush of the deep woods, chickadees scolding. Instead, she's on the Greyhound headed to the city, the hospital where her uncle lies delirious with a broken hip. Backpack full—novel, knitting, tooth brush, change of clothes—she's done this before, her mother-in-law's decline, her husband once so sick with pneumonia. Keeping vigil for the loved one pinned by tubes and wires. The hard chair, the lost hours. That's in the past, the immediate future. The driver drives, and she is settled here, cheek pressed to cold glass, attentive as the owl she glimpses hunched on a hydro pole, seven crows above it circling.

THE GOOD DAUGHTER

She's out walking that damn dog again, who knows where, how long. Have visions of a policeman at the door, she's fallen under a bus. Or the dog has dragged her under a bus, the way it pulls. We should move her into a residence—a residence, not a Home. But not with that dog, they won't take a dog like that. Never have a pet so late in life. The way she talks to it. As if it understands.

And me the only one around to see the state she's in. I go visit every single week, I call every single day, so I know, I'm the one who knows. She's failing.

She falls, I know she falls, I've seen the way she moves so stiff at times, I've seen the bruises. She says soft skin is what she has. Cracks in the sidewalks. Broken curbs. Nothing to do with the dog. Though without it she wouldn't be out in the weather, walking at all hours. Without a cell, without a way to reach me.

And what if she gets lost? Senility creeps in. When I'm her age, I'll find a place myself, I won't make trouble for my kids. Or I'll die, suddenly, doing something useful. That's the way to go. With nothing left to chance.

Her Brother

He is driving. Feet and hands go through the motions as if with a mind of their own, as if they obey the car's instructions. Signal, brake, turn.

It's dusk, and the geese are coming in to land. It's dusk, and the parking lot is almost empty. Steps outside, the air booms, rattles with wings. Thousands of birds and more coming in and the racket they make in air and on water is greater than thunder. Blackening the sky.

A woman comes out of the bush, walking quickly, hands stuffed in parka pockets. Early in the season to be wrapped in wool so tightly. And an old couple holding hands, the man leading, binoculars bouncing on his chest. About the age of his father when he died. Now his sister on the phone long distance, her complaints about their mother, her failings.

And his wife turning over in bed. She's taken to wearing a nightgown. Hot flashes, she says.

Death and disinterest. If one doesn't end things, the

other one will. He wants to be interested, to be a man with interests. Not just insurance.

They say that geese are mates for life. He stares at them, circling and landing, squabbling over a few feet of water. How do they know when it's time to leave? Time to settle down? Soon the park wardens will come on patrol. They know his name. Maybe they'll offer him coffee.

The Martyr

Comes out of the bush and a man is hanging on the fence. As if it's holding him up. Or down. Car stereo blaring.

Comes out of the bush and geese thunder overhead, cloak the black water with down. The racket. Had forgotten. And the path, how it loops and twists back on itself. The way ideas go. Memories. Desire.

Had to get out of the house for an hour, only an hour, away from the packing and unpacking, what to keep, what to toss, what to give away. Downsizing after divorce. Mum's hands shaking so badly she doesn't dare wrap the Crown Derby. Keeps saying *sorry*. Who even wants the damn china.

Mothering Mother after Father has left her. Thirty years married. Mother helpless as a child, sucking a bottle when she thinks no one is looking. All those bottles in the bin.

Comes out of the bush wishing to be anywhere but here. The man still grips the fence. Could join him, talk about music, the settling birds. They mate for life.

Put these bare palms on the wire beside his. Let the barbs prick.

The Ex Father

All he wants is the relationship, whereas she is full of questions, conclusions, conditions. At her age, she should know better.

At her age, he was already a father, was, as they say, *climbing the corporate ladder*. Her mother *falling asleep* every afternoon after school. What he came home to: dinner not made. Bed not made. Laundry spilling out of the hamper. And the scenes. The tears and accusations.

At her age she should know what silence means between a man and wife. Unspoken blame. Stifled confession.

The one time she deigned to come to his new apartment, she wouldn't take her coat off. Stood in the hall with hands on her hips, toe tapping the ceramic floor, car keys jingling. Complained about the dogs barking next door. Said, *yeah, Dad, whatever*. Said *what about the family*. The family she says he's taken from her.

She should have children of her own, and then she'll see. What it is to want. To be found wanting.

THE COUPLE

Barking of the dogs next door wakes them. And the crows. Awhile after that, a bus wheezes to a stop across the street. Everyone around them leaves, for work, for school, on vacation to the farthest East. They can stay in bed, they're on sabbatical, they're free to snuggle in their duvet's nest and dream.

Awhile after that, the nudge of feet. Then hands. Then hips. They move in silence as if not to disturb, this rental has such thin communal walls though no one else is home to hear them. Such stillness makes the most familiar magic: like walking in the first snow in the park, the trail they follow muffled. They come to the lip of the hill and let go, roll over in a flail of limbs and sheets until momentum leaves them gasping and apart. Awhile after that, one gets up to crack the blind, to let the gray light in.

The Single

Sometimes you just have to move, to feel the earth's resistance to the bones you no longer lay down lightly. Sometimes it's enough to walk under a grey sky in a January thaw, fog wisping over snow below the lowest branches of the poplars. Squirrel tracks a labyrinth to follow.

Sometimes you turn face down the portrait snapped years ago in a moment of abandon, the half smile, blouse unbuttoned to display tanned cleavage. Frame on the dresser where you see it in the morning, in the night when you turn the light on to banish spectres. You finally move it to another room.

Sometimes your phantom breast aches or the lost nipple stiffens. There's no explaining this. There's no explaining how restless you are when the day begins to darken, so early, too early. How far away the summer seems. You can't wait for tomorrow, never mind July. On long-term leave, though the treatments are, at last, thank god, over.

The *new normal*: single and single-breasted. Brittle with divorce, your sister looks at you lopsided, arms folded on her own two breasts as if she were hiding them. Protecting them. She wants to buy you padded bras, she talks of reconstruction. She can't accept you living asymmetric.

Sometimes you just have to move. Away from and toward. Travel light. Travel to the light in a land where even the alphabet is alien. Prove that you're not ready to be boxed away. Prove that you're still living.

THE TRAVELLER

Sits cross-legged by the rooftop pool, nails digging at bites on her ankles. She knows she should leave them alone. She knows she should have worn long pants last night, or doused herself with bug spray. First lesson of the tropics.

Bathed in sweat, a thin sheen on her skin as if trapped in a hot flash that never ends. And her hair, which grew back brindle (not the brown mop she was born with) crinkles in the damp. Sparks would fly if anyone should touch her.

She needs to sleep. All those hours lost in transit, a whole day lost to time zones. Hands puffy, swollen face—almost the chemo look again. The pool still, the hotel the kind that prides itself on service (though she woke to rhythmic pounding on the wall more than once last night). Maids on every floor, starched sheets, frangipani on the pillow (she thinks it's frangipani).

She dozes underneath a creaking fan, dreams helicopters thrum, guns stutter, stench of things on fire. Wakes cramped—stultified the word for how she feels. Horizon dimmed by clouds. Not clouds, smoke of slash-and-burn farming. The evening sky a scarlet haze. That's what destruction does, makes beauty from what passes. White blossoms fall. A gentle rain of ashes.

THE STUDENT

This is new. This is different. Slow boat down the Mekong: two days playing poker between rows of wooden chairs. Bets of thousands kip. Has lost about two dollars.

Hasn't eaten more than fruit. Toilet, a hole chopped through the stern. Brown water rushes underneath. Deadfall. A bloated dog. Plastic bags and bottles.

Shore crowds in, recedes: black jagged rocks or smooth brown dunes. Once a crowd of monks in saffron robes, stock still. Children chasing goats. Buffalo. Storks. An elephant, for real, hauls logs down to a barge.

Shares the platform in the bow with backpacks and six kids, blonde baby in a sling. What Mom would say to travelling like this. Boat bumps against a village dock and small girls clamber in, tote baskets of bananas, Pringles, water, beer. Their bare arms blotched with bruises, their voices a sing song.

Who he meets: Germans; Swedes; of course Americans; a drunk Israeli, burned his shin on a scooter in Phuket but still won't leave the road. An older woman travelling with a backpack on her own, an Amazon she calls herself, gives him a paperback she's finished with to read. If he could be that brave. To go and keep on going. Leave no tracks behind.

His Mother

Doesn't live in a bubble, has heard about these women of a certain age, what do they call them, cougars? "Travelling with a backpack on her own." Doesn't like the sound of that. She'll get her claws in him.

And these kids he's meeting, are they boys *and* girls? Are they more his age? He doesn't say. He doesn't say if he was by himself before the boat and after. Just a crowd of kids. He could get lost in.

Worst case scenario, his father says, *all imagination*. What does a father know? The space the baby carves inside, the space it leaves for worry to fill in. In the airport waving him good-bye, doubled over with a cramp as bad as birthing was.

Pulling on the apron strings. She knows she has to let him go and, see, she has—he's halfway round the world where it's tomorrow now and whatever night has done to him is past. How does he wash his clothes? What does he eat? *Not street food*, he promised. So far away and on his own. *A grown man*, his father says. He's not yet twenty-one. She'll bake a cake and freeze it. Tidy up his room once more, his clothes already packed for college in the fall. Sit on his bed a moment, cradle his teddy bear in her arms. Forty days to wait. And then he's home. For such a little while. Her one and only son.

The Strangers

You miss the children most in the mornings when you wake to the sound of your own breathing. No shower thundering in the pipes, no music wafting under the door of a closed room down the hall. Now all the doors are open.

You can sit in any seat at the kitchen table, back to the sunlight, read the paper, sip decaffeinated tea. The boy will not slouch in, still unshaven. Or the girls, their faces pale without the make-up they insist on wearing. They have gone to dormitory rooms, to university classes. They phone sometimes, send email. Facebook and Twitter.

You bake cookies to package to send to them. Do single loads of laundry. Visit your own mother. She drives you to the subway, her knuckles white on the steering wheel. She pulls to the stop, you already have the token in your fist. You lean to kiss the paper-thin skin of her cheek. Baby powder, imprint of lipstick. She stares straight ahead. *Come back soon,* she says as you open the door. *Don't be a stranger.*

THE NEIGHBOUR

Who has lived here long enough to watch a generation grow from infant to adult, the boy next door travelling in Asia who used to drive his Big Wheels on the sidewalk, wobble on a bike with training wheels, take his 10-speed racing up the rail trail, then learn to operate his mother's car.

Who hangs her bed sheets on the line even in winter. They come in crackling stiff, defrost on the bannister, whole house redolent with sun.

Who notices fresh squirrel tracks, rabbit tracks. Deep footsteps leading to the house next door, abandoned for no reason, boarded up. Could be the postman, meter man. Could be another neighbour checking.

Who witnesses drug transactions in the playground, young men in dark blue sports cars passing back and forth. And the van parked once a week at noon, motor idling, rocking up and down. A man, a woman, have they nowhere else to meet? The woman gets out first, tugs her clothing straight. Climbs in her red car and drives away.

Who watches. Who sees. Who notes the comings and goings, the familiar and the unfamiliar cars, the dog walkers, strollers, newspaper carriers. Who keeps herself to herself. Open laptop on her knees.

THE LOVER

Each time she swears will be the last, even as she wriggles in her seat to free the grab of nylon in her crotch, pantyhose pulled on awkward in the van, not a lot of room to move. But just enough.

Bangs her fist on the wheel, *never again*, and the horn blurts, startles an old lady on the sidewalk. Small white dog lunges right out at the car as though its red were a cape she flaunts. She brakes in time. Claws scrabble at the door, high hysteric bark. Old woman mouths *sorry* through the glass. Dog turning back to snarl.

His wife her friend, their children in the same high school classes. The two of them behave like teenagers themselves, hand notes under the dinner table, their spouses busy chatting. The passing touch. The coded conversations.

All the names she calls herself—home-wrecker, wanton, dissolute, slut. All the times she says *we have to stop doing this*, meeting in the park to talk, knowing what talk between them always leads to. His mouth. Her lips. The seats tipped back. The grey car blanket.

Each time she tells herself, *don't answer*, when her phone rings at 11:10, his morning break. She almost lets it go to voice mail, ignores the looks of co-workers at their desks, manager saying, *aren't you going to get that?* Of course she is. Of course it's him. Of course she answers *yes*. The usual place. The usual time. This hectic flush she will blame on menopause when she knows it's heat. In heat she is, and helpless.

The Other Lover

Sits in the driver's seat a good fifteen minutes after she leaves. Has put the seats back up, checked the floors for anything the twins might find, bottle caps, used kleenex. Opens windows to clear the air inside. Scent of her on his fingers.

Each time they say they're coming here to talk, no place else to go for just an hour, but the second she's in the door, they're all over the other and the only words that slip in sideways: *Here. Now. Yes.*

Toes warm from numb to normal. You can fuck, he thinks, in a van in winter almost fully dressed, but you can't make love with your socks on.

Checks his watch, reverses down the lane of snow. The *beep beep beep* a cartoon tease or warning. Which one is he? Roadrunner gets away scot free. Wolf is squashed by his own hungry wiles.

The Regular

A man comes into a bar and recognizes the regulars. Is recognized: the bartender—red hair buzz cut on top, long over the nape of her neck, white tee hiding nothing, nothing much to hide, so thin you'd miss her altogether if she stood sideways—waves, picks up a carafe, eyebrow raised. He nods yes, she pours. It's that kind of bar, trendy but not too much so.

A man comes into a bar and sits at his usual table, back to the window, facing the door, opens his Blackberry so that when she comes over he's busy with office email, can't engage in chitchat about the weather, the Leafs, whatever. Almost every weekday afternoon he's in here, often with clients, working over papers at the table, sharing a bottle of wine between them.

A man comes into a bar where there are mostly men at this hour, waiting out the worst commuter traffic. Young guy always sits on a stool, cell phone cradled to his mouth, eyes on the bartender on her rounds, how her jeans snug her ass, her tee shirt drapes small breasts she doesn't harness in a bra, they all can tell. And the man who strokes his own bare skull, a nervous tic; and yet the women fall for him, the serial monogamist, who drinks beer, not wine, *a manly man*. Who pours carefully to minimize the head. The way his father taught him. No woman with him yet.

Take my wife. Please. Some joke. Some would say the joke's on him. His son and daughter holed up in their bedrooms, wired into MySpace, headphones blocking out the sounds their mother makes. *I came, I saw, I ordered out.* Her current mantra. He's seen her cooing with their neighbour, pretends he doesn't see. Though the way she flies at him when he comes home.

Wash. Iron. Fuck. Etc.: definition of a wife. His father told that joke at their wedding reception. His new bride didn't laugh. You have to have a sense of humour, look what your life's become.

What I have done is become the man in the bar, the butt of the joke, the long face. Drains his glass, stands it neatly on the coaster. Time to go home. Face the music. *Bear the tear-stained cheat.*

The Realist

Watches. Judges. Passes sentence.

Puts names to faces to usual drinks. Knows when to interrupt a heated conversation between a man—say, the man in the corner booth and the woman with him—or disrupt a reverie that may turn into public tears—the man by the window sipping wine all by himself. *Another round?* And always with a smile.

One day dressing late for work she realized all her bras were in the dirty laundry. So went without. As if she cares they notice. Tips nearly doubled just like that. *Use what you've got to get just what you need*, Gran always said. She's always one to follow good advice.

Like *Know Yourself.* And *What You Want.* The bar is almost hers, she checks her stocks daily, investments on the rise. One more hand job after hours in the dark and the landlord will sign over. She doesn't care about his tears, betrayal of the wife she'll never meet. Herself, she's not involved. She's got what she wants, or almost.

The calculated tease. Draw the line that can't be crossed.
It's not all that hard. Life. Not rocket science.

Acknowledgements

I gratefully acknowledge the support of the Ontario Arts Council and its Writers Reserve Program.

"The Single," "The Traveller," "The Neighbour," and "The Lover" were published in *The New Quarterly*, Vol. 111 (Spring 2009). An earlier version of "The Couple" was published in the online magazine *SugarMule*, Fall 2009, and will appear in the anthology *Pith and Wry: Canadian Poets Alive*, edited by Susan McMaster.

In "The Dog-Walker": *The world is too much with us* and *For this, for everything, we are out of tune*—from "The world is too much with us," William Wordsworth, (1806); *There will be time, there will be time*—from "The Love Song of J. Alfred Prufrock," T.S. Eliot (1917).

For reading, listening, and commenting on these pieces in various drafts, I thank Susan McMaster and Michelle Berry; Lea Harper, Norma Harrs, Julie Johnston, Patricia Stone, Robyn Thomas, and Florence Treadwell; and Sarah St. Pierre and Marty Gervais.

And especially, thanks to Jim Struthers, for everything.

ABOUT THE AUTHOR

Betsy Struthers is the author of eight books of poetry and three novels and was co-editor and contributor to a book of essays about teaching poetry. This is her first book of short fiction. Winner of the 2004 Pat Lowther Memorial Award for the best book of poetry by a Canadian woman for *Still* (Black Moss), and a past president of the League of Canadian Poets, Struthers lives in Peterborough, Ontario, where she works as a freelance editor of academic texts.